Echoes of a Fractured Sun

By Julian F. Knightbridge

Table of Contents

Episode 1: The Weight of a Broken Promise

Before the cold, gray skies of Toronto, there were two distinct worlds of vibrant color in Mexico. Daniel's earliest memories were of Guadalajara, a city of bustling markets and warm, family-filled streets. The air was always thick with the scent of street food—spicy chili, charred corn, and sweet churros—and the sounds of mariachi music drifted from open doorways. His mother, Sofia, was the quiet but steady anchor in their lives. A woman of immense dignity, she carried herself with a weary grace that Daniel would only understand years later. The family's Catholicism was more a cultural tradition than a spiritual practice, a comfortable rhythm woven into the fabric of their daily life. Daniel, her quiet and observant son, and his younger brother, Chief, the boisterous and energetic counterpart, were inseparable.

Their father was a distant figure, a man who had left for "greener pastures" in Canada long before Daniel could remember his face. To Sofia, he was a ghost, a presence whose absence was a constant, gnawing pain. He was a man who lived for himself, a charming and charismatic atheist who saw life as a series of experiences to be consumed, not commitments to be kept. His leaving had been brutal, a trail of broken hearts and empty promises. He had promised to send money, to provide for them from afar, but the promises were as empty as the space he left behind. The occasional, meager remittance only highlighted his neglect, a bitter reminder that he had built a new life without them.

On the other side of Mexico, in the state of Michoacán, lived a different boy in a different world. This was Teddy, their eldest half-brother, a boy born to another woman. Teddy's mother was a woman deeply in love with a man who had promised her everything and given her nothing. When she told him she was pregnant, he simply laughed, denying the child was his. The denial was a profound trauma, a humiliation so deep it broke something inside of her. Heartbroken and unable to face the responsibility of a child alone, she had an estranged relationship with her son. She left him with his deeply religious grandmother, Abuela Esi, to raise. Abuela Esi, with a fierce, unyielding faith and a Presbyterian moral code, filled the void of his absent parents. She taught him that discipline was a form of love and that faith was the unwavering rock in a sea of chaos. Her words were scripture: "*El trabajo dignifica al hombre*," she would say. Work gives a man his dignity. His world was one of Sunday services, daily prayers, and a strict moral code that shaped him into a serious and independent young man. He was taught to stand on his own two feet, to work hard, and to trust in God's plan, a stark contrast to the communal, family-centric life Daniel and Chief knew.

The brothers, raised in two different worlds and under two different mothers, knew of each other only through hushed whispers and a few faded photographs. They were linked by blood and a man they barely knew. The silence from their father's side, a constant, quiet wound, was finally broken in the late nineties by a thick envelope with a Canadian postmark. It was a summons, an invitation to a new life. He wanted all three of them—Daniel, Chief, and Teddy—to come to Canada.

Sofia sat her sons down one afternoon, the letter on the table between them. Her hands, usually so busy, were still in her lap. Her heart, a vessel of quiet resentment, had ached for years over the father's abandonment and broken promises. This letter, full of grand pronouncements about a better life in Canada, felt like an act of supreme hypocrisy. "Your father... he wants you to come to Canada," she said, her voice strained. "He says he has a new family, a new life."

Chief, ever the child of impulse, bounced in his chair. "Canada! Like in the movies? With snow? And hockey?"

Sofia's smile was a tired, sad thing. "Yes, *mijo*. With snow." She looked at Daniel, her eyes searching his, a silent plea for him to understand. "Daniel, what do you think?"

He was on the cusp of his teenage years and felt both a hopeful flutter and a cold, creeping fear. "Will you come with us, Mama?" he asked, his voice barely a whisper. "We can all go together."

She shook her head, a single tear tracing a path down her cheek. "*Mi casa está aquí, mi hijo.* My home is here. My life is here. Your path... your path is waiting for you there." She took his hand and held it tightly. "You will be a good boy, Daniel. You will look out for your brother. You will be a man." To her, the choice was simple. She couldn't abandon her home and her mother for a man who had already proven he was untrustworthy. She would not be a third party to his new family, a silent testament to a past he had tried to erase. The boys, however, deserved a chance at a new life, a chance at the father they had never known. The familiar warmth of his family and the land of his birth were about to be replaced by the vast, cold unknown. He would cling to the small, tangible memories of home— the taste of his mother's cooking, the sound of the evening crickets, the feeling of the warm air on his skin. Decades later, Daniel would reconnect with his mother, still in Guadalajara, and he held out a quiet hope that one day, he might be able to visit her.

Episode 2: A Cold Welcome

May 1999. The air that greeted them at Toronto's Pearson Airport wasn't just cold; it was thin and sharp, smelling of jet fuel and sterile, conditioned air—a scent so alien it made Daniel's lungs ache. He clutched Chief's hand, the familiar warmth a small anchor in the overwhelming newness. Outside, the city wasn't a place of wonder but a relentless assault of concrete and glass. A symphony of car horns, screeching tires, and distant sirens replaced the gentle rhythms of Guadalajara, creating a jarring soundtrack for their arrival.

Beside them, Teddy stood as a silent, watchful presence. Daniel barely knew this older half-brother, whose quiet dignity felt both comforting and intimidating. He seemed to carry an understanding of this new reality, a premature world-weariness that Daniel found himself envying.

Their father, a man whose face was a vague memory from faded photographs, stood waiting at the arrivals gate. A new woman was by his side. She was nothing like Sofia. Her smile was a polite, careful arrangement of her lips, and her movements were detached, as if she were greeting business associates, not the sons of her husband. This was Canada, the promised land, and for Daniel, it felt less like a new beginning and more like being transplanted into barren soil.

The boys, strangers linked by a fractured bloodline, were crammed into a single, shared bedroom in a three-bedroom row house. It was a public housing project in the Jane and Finch area, a neighborhood that felt as rough and exhausted as the people in it. The walls were thin enough to hear the muffled arguments and crying babies of their neighbors, the air thick with a sense of quiet desperation. It was a world away from the vibrant, communal life they had left behind.

Episode 3: The Glass Palace

A few weeks after their arrival, on a Saturday morning thick with the promise of summer, their father announced a special trip. "Nefisa will take you boys out," he said, pressing a wad of cash into his daughter's hand. "Show them the mall. Get them something to eat."

Nefisa, their sixteen-year-old stepsister, had the weary air of a teenager assigned a chore, but there was a flicker of curiosity in her eyes. She was a bridge between their old world and this new one, a girl who moved with an easy confidence that Daniel found both fascinating and intimidating.

The word "mall" meant little to them, but the destination itself was a revelation. Yorkdale Mall in 1999 wasn't just a collection of stores; it was a cathedral of commerce under a soaring, arched glass roof that flooded the space with natural light. To Daniel, who was used to the vibrant, chaotic energy of Guadalajara's open-air *mercados*, this was something else entirely. It was clean, impossibly vast, and humming with a quiet, orderly energy.

"Whoa," Chief breathed, his head swiveling, trying to take in the two levels of storefronts that stretched into the distance. He pointed at a fountain, where water danced in time to a soft piano melody piped through invisible speakers. "It's like a palace."

Nefisa offered a small, knowing smile. "It's just a mall," she said, but she seemed pleased by his awe. "Come on, I'll show you the good stores."

She led them through the polished corridors, a confident guide in this strange new land. Teddy walked with a stiff, formal posture, his eyes taking in the sheer excess with a silent, critical gaze. This world of bright logos and expensive trinkets was a universe away from Abuela Esi's lessons on dignity and hard work. He looked at the price tag on a leather jacket in a window display and his lips tightened, a silent calculation of the hours of labor it represented.

Daniel, as always, was the quiet observer, walking a half-step behind. He watched the people: the way they walked, the casual way they carried shopping bags, the easy laughter between friends. They all seemed to possess a secret knowledge, a code of belonging that he had yet to crack.

But for Chief, it was pure magic. He pressed his face against the glass of a store called Electronics Boutique, his eyes wide at the rows of colourful video game boxes. He saw a boy his own age inside, confidently talking to the clerk, purchasing a game. It wasn't just the game Chief coveted; it was the boy's ease, his sense of ownership, the casual way he belonged in that moment.

"Okay, are you guys hungry?" Nefisa finally asked, steering them toward the food court.

The food court was a sensory assault. A dozen different smells— sweet teriyaki, greasy french fries, spicy pizza—collided in the air. It was a dizzying kaleidoscope of choice. Back home, food was what Mama made. Here, it was a hundred different options displayed under glowing plastic signs.

"What do you want?" Nefisa asked, gesturing at the sea of possibilities.

The three brothers were paralyzed by the choice. They looked at each other, a silent, shared wave of confusion passing between them.

Seeing their hesitation, Nefisa took charge. "Okay, you have to try this." She led them to a stall called New York Fries. "It's a Canadian thing."

She ordered four large containers of fries, smothered in gravy and cheese curds—a dish she called 'poutine'—and four Cokes. They found a small table in the bustling space, and for the first time since they arrived in Canada, the tension seemed to melt away.

Chief devoured his portion with unrestrained joy, the salty, savory combination a revelation to his palate. Even Teddy, after a moment of hesitation, ate with a quiet focus, a small nod of approval his only comment. Daniel ate slowly, savoring the strange, wonderful taste. In that moment, sitting at a sticky table in a loud food court, sharing a simple, greasy meal, they felt something new. It wasn't the warmth of home, not the deep, unconditional love of their mother, but it was something. A fragile, fleeting sense of normalcy.

As Nefisa talked about her school and her friends, Daniel looked from his stepsister's confident face to Teddy's guarded expression, to Chief's unburdened smile. He looked up at the vast glass ceiling, at the endless stream of people, and a single thought crystallized in his mind. This was the life their father had chosen. A life of dazzling palaces and endless choices, a world so bright and overwhelming it threatened to swallow them whole. And for a moment, he felt a dangerous, unfamiliar flicker of hope that maybe, just maybe, they could find a place in it too.

Episode 4: The Second Table

The morning after they arrived, the boys woke to a house that was already humming with a life that did not include them. The breakfast was a quick, impersonal affair: slices of toasted white bread with margarine and a box of cereal Daniel didn't recognize. After the meager meal, as their father left for work and the other children prepared for their day, Maria approached them, a cloth and a bucket in her hands.

"The floors need a good cleaning," she said, her tone matter-of-fact, not unkind, but with the unmistakable air of an order being given. "You can start in the kitchen."

There was a beat of stunned silence. In Guadalajara, chores were part of the family rhythm, but this felt different. This was a task assigned, a debt to be paid for their own presence. Chief looked confused, as if he'd misheard. Daniel's face remained passive, but a cold knot formed in his stomach. It was Teddy who responded, his voice even. "Yes, of course." He took the bucket from her, his expression unreadable. For the next two hours, they worked on their hands and knees, the scent of lemon-scented cleaner filling their nostrils. It was their second day in the promised land, and they were paying for their keep.

That evening, the true geography of their new life was made clear. The three-bedroom row house was impossibly crowded, a chaotic dance of eleven people. When Maria announced dinner was ready, a frantic rush to the dining room began. Their father took his place at the head of the table, Maria at the other end. Nefisa and the other children squeezed onto the remaining chairs, a loud, laughing tangle of limbs. There was no room for the three new arrivals.

"Boys, you can eat in the living room," Maria said, already handing them plates heavy with food. "Just be careful with the carpet."

It wasn't a suggestion. It was a logistical necessity that felt like a decree. They were not part of the inner circle. They were satellites, orbiting the warm, bright star of the family table. Daniel, Teddy, and Chief took their plates and retreated to the living room, sitting on the floor with their backs against the sofa. From there, they had a clear view of the dining room, a tableau of a family they could see but not join.

The meal was lamb chops with mint sauce, boiled potatoes, and steamed green beans. To Maria, it was a generous offering. To the boys, sitting on the floor, it was the strange, bland food of exile. The sounds from the other room—the clinking of cutlery, the bursts of laughter, the easy, overlapping chatter—washed over them, a language of belonging they weren't invited to speak.

Chief poked at the pale meat, his nose wrinkling. "What is this?" he whispered to Daniel.

"Lamb," Daniel whispered back, though the word meant nothing to him. He missed the comforting heat of chili, the sharp tang of lime, the earthy scent of cilantro. He missed his mother's hands in the kitchen.

Teddy, as always, was a fortress of self-control. He ate with a stoic determination, his back straight, as if to prove that the indignity of their situation could not touch him. He shot Chief a warning look, a silent, sharp command: *Be grateful. Be invisible.*

Daniel watched his father at the head of the other table, holding court. He laughed at a joke one of the younger children told. He asked Maria about her day. His attention was a spotlight, and it was aimed squarely away from the three sons sitting on the floor in the next room.

"Daniel, you're very quiet over there!" Maria called out, her voice a little too bright.

The entire dining table turned to look at them. The conversation stopped. For a moment, they were on display. The question felt less like an invitation and more like a test. "It's good, thank you," Daniel said softly, his eyes on his plate.

"He likes to read," their father chimed in, his voice carrying across the space. "Very smart."

The spotlight moved on. The chatter resumed. The boys were once again forgotten.

Finally, Chief could take it no more. "I don't like it," he whispered, pushing his plate away. His voice, meant to be a secret between the brothers, carried in a lull in the conversation.

In the dining room, a fork clattered onto a plate. The laughter died.

"What was that?" their father asked, his voice dangerously calm. He stood up and walked to the archway that separated the two rooms, looming over the three boys on the floor.

Chief shrank back. "Nothing, Papá."

"I heard you," his father said, his eyes cold. "You will be grateful for the food this family provides you. You will be grateful for the roof over your head."

"I'm sorry, Papá," Chief mumbled, tears welling in his eyes.

The apology hung in the air, but it didn't fix anything. The line had been drawn, not in sand, but in the very architecture of the house. They weren't just at a second table; they were in a different room entirely. Daniel looked at his brothers, then at the family in the other room, and understood with a cold, sinking certainty that in this house, they would always be hungry here.

Episode 5: The Factory Floor

The indignity of the second table and the sting of their father's coldness settled into a quiet, motivating anger. It was Teddy, driven by Abuela Esi's deeply ingrained lessons on the dignity of work, who led the charge. He wouldn't allow them to be dependents, living on the scraps of their father's new life. They had to earn their own way.

Through a contact from a man who attended the same church as Maria's family, Teddy secured them jobs. They were weekend and after-school shifts at a plastics factory, a place of mind-numbing, grueling labor. For hours, they stood on a concrete floor under the glare of fluorescent lights, the air thick with the acrid smell of heated plastic, pulling freshly molded items from hot machines. The noise was a constant roar, and their hands, unaccustomed to the repetitive motion, quickly became blistered and raw.

When their first paycheques arrived, they weren't handed to the boys. Their father intercepted them. "I will set up bank accounts for you," he announced, as if it were an act of great generosity. "It is important to learn to save. Maria and I will manage the accounts for you, to make sure the money is safe."

The promise of "safety" felt more like a cage. The boys never saw a bank statement, never held a bank card. They worked, came home exhausted, and their earnings vanished into a financial black hole controlled by their father and stepmother. The exhaustion from the factory was now compounded by a corrosive sense of powerlessness.

After two months of this, Teddy had had enough. He cornered his father in the kitchen one evening after dinner. Daniel and Chief watched from the living room, a familiar sense of dread tightening their chests.

"Papá, I need access to my bank account," Teddy said, his voice respectful but firm. "We need money for things. For clothes."

"We provide you with everything you need," his father replied, not looking up from the newspaper he was reading. "Your money is being saved for your future."

"What future?" Teddy pressed, his voice rising slightly. "We are working now. We are earning money now. It is our money. I am seventeen years old. I have a right to it."

"You have a right to what I give you," his father snapped, finally putting the paper down. His eyes were cold. "You are living under my roof. Do not forget that."

"I have not forgotten," Teddy said, his voice low and intense. "But I will not be treated like a child. I want my bank card."

The standoff was quiet but absolute. It was a battle of wills, and for the first time, their father seemed to realize that Teddy would not back down. With a heavy, theatrical sigh of annoyance, he finally relented. "Fine," he spat. "I will speak to the bank. But do not come crying to me when you have wasted it all."

A week later, Teddy was given his bank card. It was a monumental victory, but a hollow one. When he checked the balance at an ATM, a significant portion of what he had calculated he'd earned was simply gone—siphoned off for "household expenses" he had never been consulted on.

With the money he managed to secure, he took his brothers to a discount clothing store. It wasn't the triumphant shopping spree they had dreamed of. It was a careful, calculated exercise in necessity. Teddy bought sturdy work boots. Chief got a new pair of sneakers, Daniel a warm winter coat. The purchases felt less like a choice and more like a reclamation of something that had been stolen.

They pooled what little was left in a tin box. As Christmas approached, they sat in their room and made a list of eleven names. The number was daunting. The amount of cash in the box was pitiful.

"It's not enough," Chief said, his voice quiet with dawning disappointment.

"We will get what we can," Teddy said, his voice tight with a frustration he tried to conceal.

But Daniel, watching his brother's forced optimism, knew the truth. They hadn't just failed to earn enough; their earnings had been taken from them. They had been set up to fail. The dream of a Canadian

Christmas, one where they could stand as equals, was already turning to ash.

Episode 6: The Coldest Christmas

Christmas morning arrived not with a sense of joy, but with a quiet, suffocating dread. The house smelled of pine and cinnamon, an artificial cheerfulness that felt like a mockery. Downstairs, the living room was a mountain of brightly wrapped presents under a glittering tree. Maria's children were a blur of joyous energy, tearing into boxes with squeals of delight, their laughter echoing in the tense silence where the three brothers stood.

Daniel, Chief, and Teddy sat on the periphery, relegated once again to the floor by the archway. They were spectators at a feast to which they had not been invited. They had nothing to offer. The few, meager dollars left in their tin box after their father's "management" of their earnings had been enough for a single, shared gift for Maria and their father—a generic box of chocolates—and nothing more. They had wrapped it carefully, a pathetic offering against the tide of presents flooding the room.

Their father, a man who valued appearances above all else, watched the proceedings with a proprietary smile. But his eyes kept flicking over to the three boys sitting silently, their hands empty. Daniel could feel his father's irritation growing, a low hum of energy in the room. It was a slight against his new family, a glaring, public reminder of the old life he had so desperately tried to erase.

The gift-giving wound down. Piles of discarded wrapping paper littered the floor. The other children were happily playing with their new toys. The silence from the boys' corner of the room became unbearable.

Suddenly, their father's voice cut through the air, low and dangerous. "Why are you two just sitting there?" he asked, his gaze fixed on Chief and Teddy. "Why don't you have gifts for the children?"

Teddy, the oldest, the one who had always carried the weight of their father's sins, stood up. His face was a mask of quiet fury, but his voice was steady. "Father, we bought you and Maria a gift." He gestured to the small, lonely box of chocolates under the tree. "We did not have enough money for everyone. You know this. We worked, but..."

"Don't you talk back to me!" their father snapped, his voice rising, the carefully constructed festive atmosphere shattering like glass. He took a step toward them. "You think you can just come here and take, take, take? Live in my house, eat my food, and not give anything back? You are a shame to this family!"

Chief, his face pale and crumpling, began to cry. "*Perdón, Papá,*" he sobbed. "We're sorry. We tried."

But the apology was gasoline on the fire. Their father's voice was filled with a cold, absolute fury that seemed to suck all the air from the room. "Sorry is not enough! Get out! *¡Fuera de aquí!* Get out of my house!"

The words hung in the air, unbelievable and final. Maria looked on, her face a mixture of shock and something that looked unnervingly like relief. Nefisa stared, her mouth slightly open. The other children fell silent, their new toys forgotten.

Teddy didn't plead. He didn't argue. He simply straightened his shoulders, a lifetime of his father's betrayals hardening his face into a mask of stone. He walked to the closet, pulled out his and Chief's thin coats, and took his younger brother by the hand.

Daniel watched them leave from the living room window, a knot of pure terror tightening in his stomach. He saw Chief's small, heaving shoulders, Teddy's rigid back. Then, the undeniable sound of the front door slamming shut, followed by the quiet, heavy footsteps of two boys walking away into the biting Canadian winter. They were just children, cast out into the cold with nowhere to go.

He was alone now, in a house that felt more alien than ever, with a father who seemed to be slipping further away, consumed by the demands of his new life. The silence in the house after his brothers left was deafening. In that moment, Daniel learned a new kind of survival. He learned to be invisible, to take up as little space as possible, to anticipate every mood shift. He would later realize that the trauma of that night, the visceral feeling of being discarded and unwanted, was a wound that would never truly heal. It was the moment that would forever define his relationship with his father—a man who had chosen a new life over his old one, a man who had chosen to abandon his children not once, but twice.

Episode 7: Covenant House

The slam of their father's door was a sound of absolute finality. The Toronto cold that hit them was a physical blow, stealing the air from their lungs. For a few moments, Teddy and Chief just stood on the frozen sidewalk, two ghosts expelled from a life that was never truly theirs. Christmas lights on the neighboring houses blinked with a cruel cheerfulness, illuminating the small puffs of their breath in the frigid air.

Chief's sobs were small, choked things. He huddled against Teddy, his thin coat useless against the wind that whipped down the suburban street. "Teddy, I'm scared," he whispered, his teeth chattering. "Where do we go?"

Teddy, barely an adult himself at seventeen, felt a cold terror that was sharper than the wind. He was the older brother. He was supposed to have a plan. But all he had was the searing image of his father's rage and the weight of Chief's small, trembling hand in his own. He looked up and down the quiet street. The houses, moments ago just buildings, now seemed like fortresses with their warm lights and closed doors. They were utterly, terrifyingly alone.

He remembered the factory, the long bus rides that took them through the heart of the city. He remembered seeing a police station downtown. It was the only anchor he could think of. "We're going to find help," he said, his voice more confident than he felt. "Come on."

They walked for what felt like hours, their feet growing numb, following the main roads toward the distant glow of the downtown core. They finally found a payphone, its plastic receiver cold as ice against Teddy's ear. He fumbled with the coins, his fingers stiff and clumsy, and called the police.

The voice on the other end was professional, detached, and delivered a blow more chilling than the winter air. Because they were sixteen and seventeen, the officer explained, their parents were not legally obligated to keep them. They weren't children in the eyes of the law; they were a problem with no easy solution. The officer provided a list of resources, his tone offering no comfort, only procedure. The final suggestion was a youth shelter downtown: Covenant House.

A police cruiser arrived a short time later, its flashing lights painting the street in strokes of red and blue. The ride downtown was silent, the two brothers huddled in the back seat, the plastic partition a barrier between them and the world of rules that had just failed them so completely.

Covenant House was an intimidating fortress of brick and glass on a busy downtown street. But the light spilling from its windows was a beacon. Inside, it smelled of industrial cleaner, coffee, and a faint, underlying scent of collective sorrow. A woman with tired eyes and a kind smile greeted them, took their names, and led them to a small intake room.

They were given warm beds in a dormitory filled with other kids, a brotherhood and sisterhood of the rejected, each with their own tale of a door slammed shut. They were given a hot meal—a simple stew that tasted like the most delicious food they had ever eaten. For the first time in hours, the gnawing fear in their stomachs began to subside.

They spent the next three months in that strange limbo. Teddy, clinging to the discipline Abuela Esi had drilled into him, found his resolve. Her voice was a constant echo in his mind, reminding him that faith was an anchor and education was a ladder. This, he knew, was a test. He made sure they both continued to attend Brendan Heights Secondary School, taking the bus every morning from the shelter, their homelessness a secret shame they carried with their books.

Chief, however, retreated into a shell of sullen silence. The boisterous energy that had defined him was extinguished, replaced by a quiet, watchful anger. The trauma of that Christmas Day had broken something in him. While Teddy saw the shelter as a temporary stop on the path forward, Chief saw it as just another version of the second table—a place where he was an outsider, a charity case. He was no longer a boy in a palace of glass; he was a ghost in a house of ghosts, and the rift between him and the brother who was trying so desperately to save him had already begun to form.

Episode 8: The Lifeline

Their lifeline came in the form of a Trinidadian social worker, a kind but no-nonsense woman named Mrs. Peters who saw past their trauma to the potential beneath. She worked tirelessly for them, navigating the labyrinthine bureaucracy of social assistance. After three months in the shelter, she delivered the news: she had secured them a small basement apartment on Whitley Avenue in North York. It wasn't much, but it was a home. It was theirs.

They moved in with nothing but the clothes on their backs and a few items donated by the shelter. The apartment was small and damp, with low ceilings and a single window that looked out onto the feet of passersby. But to Teddy, it was a kingdom.

A few weeks later, another angel appeared. Bertha Jo Herriott, a teacher from their high school, had noticed their prolonged absence and, through her own quiet investigation, finally tracked them down. When she arrived at their bare apartment and heard the full story of that Christmas Day, she stood in the doorway with tears in her eyes.

The next day, she returned with her husband, Gabe, their car filled with donations. They brought a small dining table with two chairs, plates, cutlery, and pots and pans—the basic architecture of a home. But Bertha Jo offered more than just things. She opened the door to her own family.

"You will come for dinner," she said, her voice leaving no room for argument. "Every Sunday. My children, Kristina and James, would love to meet you."

It was an offer of a stable, loving family that was utterly alien to the brothers. And it was an offer Teddy desperately needed. He accepted it without hesitation. He found in the Herriotts' warm, noisy home a sanctuary. He talked with Gabe about school and his future, and in James, he found a brother he could speak to without the heavy weight of their shared trauma. The Herriotts became his surrogate family, a vital anchor that kept him grounded in a world that had tried to cast him adrift.

Chief, however, couldn't accept it. He went to their house for dinner once, a polite but silent guest at the table. The kindness felt like charity, another reminder of what he didn't have. The happy family dynamic felt like a judgment on his own broken one. He refused to go back.

"They're good people, Chief," Teddy pleaded one evening, after returning from a Sunday dinner at the Herriotts'.

"They feel sorry for us," Chief mumbled, refusing to meet his eyes. He was sitting on the edge of his mattress, staring at the blank wall. "I don't want anyone feeling sorry for me."

"It's not pity, it's kindness," Teddy insisted. "They want to help."

"I don't need their help!" Chief shot back, his voice raw. "I don't need anyone's help."

The difference—Teddy's ability to accept help and Chief's inability to—became another crack in their already fragile foundation. Teddy saw the Herriotts as a lifeline, a chance to build a new, better life. Chief saw them as a reminder of his own powerlessness, another version of the second table. The small basement apartment, once a shared kingdom, was now divided territory, and the two brothers, once united in their loss, were beginning to drift apart on separate, lonely seas.

Episode 9: The Five-Finger Discount

For a few months, they made it work. Teddy got a job washing dishes in a small restaurant, his nights filled with the smell of grease and the clatter of plates. His meager earnings, combined with their social assistance, were just enough to cover rent and groceries. He was always tired, but it was the satisfying exhaustion of providing, of building something.

Chief, however, was unraveling. The silence that had begun at the shelter morphed into a reckless energy. He started spending more and more time at the Yorkdale Mall, not with the wide-eyed wonder of their first visit, but with a new, calculating gaze. He watched the other kids, the ones with money to spare, and a bitter resentment began to fester.

His first crime was not a plan; it was an impulse born of that bitterness. Standing in a candy store, surrounded by bright colors and sweet smells he couldn't afford, he saw a moment of distraction. A clerk turned to help another customer. His hand, acting on its own volition, moved with a speed that surprised him, tucking a chocolate bar into his jacket pocket. His heart hammered against his ribs, a frantic drumbeat of terror and exhilaration. He walked out, the automatic doors sliding open into the cool air, and he didn't stop walking for ten blocks.

That night, in the privacy of their small apartment, he ate the chocolate bar. It was sweet, but the taste of control was sweeter. It was a dangerous taste, and he found himself craving more.

The thefts escalated. A video game from Electronics Boutique. A CD from a music store. Small things, easily concealed, but each one was a small victory against the world that had rejected him. He wasn't a charity case; he was a provider, in his own way. He was taking what he felt he was owed.

Teddy found the stash under Chief's mattress one evening while looking for a missing textbook. A pile of stolen goods, still in their plastic wrapping. He sank onto the edge of his own bed, the stolen game heavy in his hand. He felt a profound pain, a sorrow that went deeper than just the fear of being caught. He had his own pain, his own memories of their father's cruelty, but he always found refuge in the words of Abuela Esi, in the quiet certainty that God had a plan.

He believed this hardship was a test of their character, a fire to forge them into stronger men. But Chief was not forging; he was breaking.

The confrontation that followed wasn't loud or violent like their father's rages; it was quiet and heartbreaking.

"Chief, what is this?" Teddy asked, his voice barely a whisper. "Where did you get this?"

"It's just stuff," Chief mumbled, refusing to meet his eyes. "Who cares?"

"I care!" Teddy's voice cracked with an anguish that was deeper than anger. "We care! After everything Bertha Jo did? After everything we've been through? This is not God's plan for us, Chief. This is not the path. We lose this apartment, we lose everything. We go back to the shelter."

"We have nothing anyway," Chief shot back, a flash of his old anger returning.

"We have this!" Teddy gestured around the small, dim room, at the very table Bertha Jo had given them. "We have each other. We have a chance to be good men. Don't throw it away for... for this."

But Chief couldn't see it as a chance. He saw it as a prison, another version of being powerless. He saw his brother, speaking of God's plan while working himself to the bone for a life that was barely a life at all. He saw the kindness of the Herriotts as a constant reminder of their own failure.

Teddy lived in constant fear of a knock on the door, of seeing his younger brother in handcuffs. The strain became a rift between them. The bond that had been forged in shared loss began to fray under the weight of Teddy's impossible responsibility and Chief's unaddressed pain. The final separation was not yet a reality, but in the tense silence that filled their small apartment that night, it felt inevitable.

Episode 10: The Quiet Admission

The final straw came on a Tuesday. Teddy was elbow-deep in greasy water at the restaurant, the roar of the kitchen a familiar backdrop to his thoughts, when the manager called him to the phone. It was a police officer. Chief had been caught shoplifting at the Eaton Centre.

A cold dread washed over Teddy, colder than the dirty dishwater. The Eaton Centre. Not the local mall, but the massive, glass-roofed heart of downtown. Chief was getting bolder, more reckless. Teddy dried his hands, apologized to his manager, and took the bus downtown, his mind a maelstrom of prayer and fear.

He found Chief in a small, sterile security office in the mall's basement. His younger brother was slumped in a chair, his face a mixture of sullen defiance and barely concealed terror. A weary-looking mall security guard stood by the door, and a uniformed police officer was filling out paperwork at a desk.

"Are you his legal guardian?" the officer asked, looking up at Teddy, his gaze impassive.

"I'm his brother," Teddy said, his voice quiet.

The officer sighed, a sound of practiced patience. "I understand that. But are you his legal guardian? Are you over eighteen?"

"No. I'm seventeen."

The officer put down his pen. "Then there's nothing you can do here, son. Your brother has been caught stealing merchandise valued at over two hundred dollars. He's being charged. We need to speak to his legal guardian. A parent."

The word "parent" hung in the air like a judgment. Teddy's mind flashed to his father, to the rage in his eyes on Christmas Day. Calling him was not an option. It would be like throwing gasoline on a fire.

"We don't... we don't have anyone to call," Teddy said, the admission tasting like ash in his mouth.

The officer's expression softened for a fraction of a second. He had seen this story before. "Look," he said, his voice a little gentler. "Because he's a minor, he'll likely be released with a desk appearance ticket and a future court date. But you can't take responsibility for him. You're a kid yourself. There's nothing for you to do here."

Helpless. The word echoed in Teddy's soul. He had tried so hard to be a father, a provider, a guardian. But in the eyes of the world, in the eyes of the law, he was just a boy. He couldn't protect Chief. He couldn't even sign a piece of paper for him. He looked at his younger brother, who refused to meet his gaze, and felt a profound, bottomless sense of failure. He had to leave him there.

The long walk back to their apartment on Whitley Avenue was a funeral march. Each step was heavy with the weight of his decision. He thought of Abuela Esi's words about dignity and hard work. He thought of his prayers, his belief that God was testing them. But what if the test wasn't to see if he could save his brother, but to see if he could save himself? He couldn't let Chief's descent pull him under too. He had to let go.

He arrived at the empty apartment. The table from Bertha Jo stood in the corner, a monument to a life they had failed to build together. With a heavy heart, Teddy packed a small bag with his clothes and his few books.

Chief arrived hours later, the desk appearance ticket crumpled in his pocket. He saw the bag by the door and froze.

"I have to go, Chief," Teddy said, his voice devoid of anger, filled only with a vast, weary sadness. "I can't... I can't do this anymore. I can't save you."

"So you're just leaving me?" Chief's voice cracked, the defiant mask crumbling to reveal the terrified boy beneath. "Like he did?"

The comparison was a knife in Teddy's heart, but it didn't change his mind. "I'm not him," he said quietly. "I'm trying to survive. And I can't do it if I'm waiting for a knock on the door every night. I love you. But I have to save myself."

To Chief, it was the echo of Christmas Day all over again. Another door closing, another brother walking away. The rift between them was now a canyon. Teddy walked out of the apartment, leaving Chief alone with the stolen goods, the court summons, and the ruins of their shared life. They were left to navigate their broken new world alone.

Episode 11: A Different Cage

The years after his brothers' departure blurred into a careful, suffocating routine. Daniel perfected the art of invisibility. He spoke when spoken to, kept his grades high, and took up as little emotional space as possible. He heard whispers about his brothers—that Teddy was in college, that Chief was in and out of trouble—but they were like characters in a book he was no longer allowed to read. He was a ghost in his father's house, a silent observer of a family that was not his own.

Around 2004, when Daniel was on the cusp of his sixteenth birthday, his father announced they were moving. They were leaving the cramped, noisy world of the Jane and Finch housing project for a new, larger house in Brampton. To his father and Maria, it was a symbol of success, a step up into the quiet, manicured world of the suburbs.

The new house was spacious, with a backyard and a finished basement. For the first time, Daniel had his own room. But the extra space didn't feel like freedom; it felt like a bigger, emptier cage. The muted colors and sharp edges of the housing project were replaced by beige walls and beige carpets. The constant, chaotic energy of their old neighborhood was gone, replaced by the distant hum of lawnmowers and the oppressive silence of suburban nights. The move didn't change his status; it just gave his loneliness more room to echo.

For a long time, Daniel had held onto a quiet admiration for Teddy. He saw in his older brother a figure of stability, a man who had survived their father's cruelty and forged his own path through sheer force of will. He didn't know the full story of the shelter or the crushing weight of responsibility Teddy had carried for Chief, only that his brother had survived and was now succeeding in college. Teddy was everything their father was not: disciplined, responsible, and honorable.

One evening, his father called him into the living room. Maria was there, sitting on the new sofa, her expression neutral.

"Daniel," his father began, without preamble. "You will go live with Teddy."

The words were not a suggestion; they were a command. Daniel stared at him, stunned.

"He is a disciplined young man," his father continued, a note of pride in his voice, as if he were somehow responsible for Teddy's success. "He is in college. He has his own apartment. He will teach you to be responsible. It is time you learned to be a man."

Daniel looked from his father's impassive face to Maria's. He saw no concern for him in their eyes, only a convenient solution to a long-standing problem. They were not sending him to Teddy for his own good; they were sending him away. He was the last ghost from the past, and they were finally exorcising him.

A thousand emotions flooded Daniel at once: a familiar, cold dread at the thought of Teddy's rigid rules, but also a surprising, hopeful flutter. It was a chance to escape this sterile house. It was a chance to reconnect with the one brother he had always looked up to. It was, perhaps, a chance to finally find a place where he belonged.

"Okay," Daniel said, his voice barely a whisper.

He packed a single bag that night, the few clothes and books he owned. As he looked around the beige, impersonal room that had been his for less than a year, he felt nothing. He was leaving one cage for another, but this time, at least, the keeper of the cage would be his brother.

Episode 12: The Rules of the House

Daniel arrived at his brother's apartment with his single bag and a heart full of conflicting emotions. The building was a nondescript, low-rise brick building in a quiet, working-class neighborhood. It was a world away from the manicured lawns of Brampton and the chaotic energy of Jane and Finch.

Teddy opened the door before Daniel could knock, as if he had been waiting. He was taller than Daniel remembered, and leaner. The years of fending for himself had sharpened the angles of his face and put a permanent weariness in his eyes. He didn't smile or hug Daniel; he simply nodded.

"You're here," Teddy said, his voice low and serious. He took Daniel's bag and set it down inside. "Welcome."

Teddy's apartment was a sanctuary of order. It was small, meticulously clean, and smelled of coffee and paper. Books lined one wall, not crammed onto shelves, but arranged neatly by subject. There were no decorations, no photographs, no clutter. It was the living space of a man who had declared war on chaos and was winning.

"This is not your father's house," Teddy said, turning to face Daniel. His gaze was direct and unflinching. "The rules here are different. I am not your father. I will not just give you things. But I will give you a chance."

He walked Daniel through the small apartment, laying out the terms of his new existence. "You will have a place to sleep," he said, gesturing to a small, clean mattress on the floor of the living room. "You will have food to eat. You will have a quiet place to study. In return, you will contribute. You will get a part-time job after school. You will pay for your own expenses. You will do your share of the chores. There is a schedule on the refrigerator. You will follow it."

He paused, his eyes holding Daniel's. "There is no room for laziness here, Daniel. No room for excuses. We don't have anyone else to catch us if we fall. Do you understand?"

Daniel nodded, the words lodging in his throat. He understood the logic. He saw the clear, hard path to a future where he wouldn't be at the mercy of others' whims. He saw the strength in his brother's discipline, the same strength he had admired from afar. For a while, he thought, he could thrive in this structure. He could learn.

But as he looked around the sterile, orderly apartment, at the rigid lines and the empty spaces, he felt a familiar sensation. The hope that had fluttered in his chest on the drive over was being replaced by the cold reality of another set of rules, another set of expectations he was terrified to fail.

The cage had changed, but it was still a cage.

Episode 13: The Breaking Point

For the first few months, the arrangement worked. Daniel, terrified of failing, adhered to Teddy's rigid schedule. He got a part-time job at a grocery store, did his chores without complaint, and kept his grades up. But the sterile order of his brother's apartment began to wear on him.

The small space became even more crowded with the arrival of Mr. Henderson, a history teacher from their high school. A kind, witty man originally from England, Mr. Henderson was in the early stages of Multiple Sclerosis, a condition that was beginning to affect his mobility but not his sharp mind. He had known Teddy through a school mentorship program and, needing an affordable and accessible place to live, had decided to pool his resources with the brothers.

Their combined income allowed them to move into a three-bedroom apartment. It was a step up, a place with more room and light. Daniel finally had his own room, a small space with a door he could close. But instead of using the privacy for his studies, he found a different kind of refuge: video games.

He bought a used console with money from his grocery store job. It started as a simple escape, a way to decompress after a long day of school and work. But soon, the digital worlds of fantasy and combat became more real and compelling to him than his own life. The clear objectives, the sense of power, the immediate rewards—it was everything his own life lacked. Schoolwork seemed dull and pointless in comparison. His grades, once a source of pride, began to slip.

Teddy, who viewed any deviation from the path of relentless self-improvement as a moral failure, saw the video games as a dangerous poison. He would come home from his own long day of college classes and work to find Daniel bathed in the flickering glow of the television, his homework untouched.

The arguments started small. "Daniel, you need to finish your homework," Teddy would say, his voice tight with frustration.

"I'll do it later," Daniel would reply, his eyes not leaving the screen.

Mr. Henderson often found himself an unwilling observer of their growing conflict. He would sit at the kitchen table, nursing a cup of tea, and listen to the tension escalate. He saw the desperation behind Teddy's discipline and the quiet rebellion in Daniel's defiance.

One evening, the simmering conflict boiled over. Report cards had come out, and Daniel's once-stellar marks had plummeted. Teddy confronted him, the damning piece of paper trembling in his hand.

"What is this, Daniel?" Teddy demanded, his voice low and intense. "You are throwing everything away for these stupid games!"

"They're not stupid!" Daniel retorted, his own voice rising with a year of pent-up frustration. "It's the only thing I like! It's the only thing that's mine!"

"Your future is what is yours! Your education!" Teddy shot back. "This is a luxury we cannot afford! Tired is a luxury we cannot afford! Do you think this is a game?"

"It's better than this!" Daniel yelled, gesturing around the apartment. "Your schedules and your rules! I'm tired of it! I'm tired of being a project!"

To Daniel, it felt like a final judgment, another set of impossible rules he was doomed to fail. That night, he lay awake, the walls of his small room closing in. He couldn't do it anymore. He needed to breathe. He needed to make a mistake, to be messy, to fail on his own terms.

The next morning, before the sun had risen, before his brother woke to enforce the day's schedule, Daniel packed a small bag. He left a brief, inadequate note on the kitchen counter, thanking his brother but explaining, vaguely, that he needed to find his own path.

He slipped out of the apartment, the quiet click of the door echoing in the pre-dawn stillness. Mr. Henderson, awake early, saw him go from the kitchen window but said nothing. He simply watched the boy walk away, a solitary figure disappearing into a city that was just beginning to stir, a vast, indifferent landscape waiting to swallow him whole.

Episode 14: The Allure of the Game

The word Daniel repeated in his mind as he walked away from his brother's apartment was *freedom*. But freedom, he quickly discovered, felt a lot like fear and tasted like the metallic tang of an empty stomach. The paltry sum of cash from his grocery store job was enough for a few nights in a dilapidated boarding house in a forgotten corner of the city, a place where the hallways smelled of stale cigarette smoke, boiled cabbage, and desperation.

He learned the rhythm of this new life quickly: the dehumanizing lines at the social welfare office where he learned to keep his eyes down and his answers vague; the gnawing ache of real hunger that became a constant companion; and the corrosive shame of his own powerlessness. The world was no longer a series of rules to follow or rebel against; it was a sheer cliff face he couldn't find a foothold on.

His first crime was not a plan; it was an impulse born of pure need. He was standing in a brightly lit grocery store, a palace of abundance he couldn't afford, his stomach a hollow pit. He saw a moment of distraction. A cashier looked away, a stock boy turned his back. His hand, acting on its own volition, moved with a speed that surprised him, tucking a plastic-wrapped pack of instant noodles under his jacket.

His heart hammered against his ribs, a frantic drumbeat of terror and exhilaration. He walked out, the automatic doors sliding open into the cold air, and he didn't stop walking for ten blocks, the fear that a hand would grab his shoulder propelling him forward.

That night, in the privacy of his grim little room, he cooked the noodles on a stolen hot plate. They were bland, salty, and tasted like nothing he had ever eaten before. They tasted of control.

The thrill wasn't just in getting away with it; it was the intoxicating rush of imposing his will on a world that had only ever imposed its will on him. For the first time since he was a small boy in Guadalajara, he felt like he had made a decision that was truly his own. He had seen a problem—hunger—and he had solved it. It was a dangerous taste, and he found himself craving more. The game had begun.

Episode 15: The Craft

The taste of control was addictive. Hunger was no longer the primary motivation; the game was. Daniel began to apply the discipline Teddy had tried so hard to instill in him, not to homework, but to his new craft. Shoplifting became a science.

He was meticulous, patient, observant. He would spend hours in a store without taking anything, simply watching. He learned the blind spots of security cameras, the tired routines of loss prevention officers, the precise moment a cashier's attention was diverted. He learned the art of blending in, of moving with a quiet confidence that drew no suspicion. He became a ghost in the aisles, accumulating small victories that translated into food, a warmer coat, and a growing sense of mastery over his environment.

He fell in with a loose-knit group of young men from the boarding house and the surrounding streets. They were like him: adrift, invisible, and trying to survive in the city's margins. They called themselves the "Shadows," and in their shared risk, Daniel found a twisted kind of camaraderie, a sense of belonging he hadn't felt since

Chief was by his side. They shared tips, looked out for each other, and sometimes collaborated on small scores.

One of the Shadows, a charismatic older guy named Marcus, saw something different in Daniel. It wasn't just desperation; it was a quiet precision, a calculated approach that stood out from the others' clumsy impulsiveness. Marcus took Daniel under his wing. He wasn't just a thief; he was a philosopher of the streets.

"The game is simple," Marcus said one night, the two of them sitting on a fire escape overlooking the glittering, indifferent city. "Everyone's taking something. The bankers in their suits, the politicians with their smiles. They just have better lawyers. We're just more honest about it."

Marcus taught him how to turn a quick profit, how to spot an opportunity, how to talk his way out of a tight spot. Daniel, with his quiet intelligence and natural charm, proved to be a natural player. He learned to be a performer, using his polite demeanor to disarm clerks and his observant nature to plan his scores with an unnerving precision.

But the small scores only whetted his appetite. He saw the flash of expensive watches, the gleam of luxury cars, and a hunger grew in him—not just for money, but for the life it represented. The life of effortless power his father had chosen over him. The game was getting bigger, and he was ready to level up.

Episode 16: The First Arrest

The hunger for a bigger score led Daniel to a downtown electronics store, a place filled with the kind of high-value, easily fenced items Marcus had taught him to look for. This wasn't about stealing noodles anymore; this was about profit. This was leveling up.

He did his homework, casing the store for two days, mapping the camera locations and learning the staff's routines. He identified his target: a stack of new-release video games and a display of high-end headphones. He walked in on a busy afternoon, a ghost in a sea of shoppers, his heart beating a steady, confident rhythm. The game was on.

He moved with his practiced, fluid grace, slipping the items into a specially lined bag. He was calm, focused, his senses alive. He felt the familiar intoxicating rush of control. He turned to leave, his path to the door clear.

And then, a hand clamped down on his shoulder.

"Sir, I need you to come with me."

The voice was young, firm. The confidence that had buoyed Daniel moments before evaporated, replaced by a surge of pure, cold panic. The security guard was new, a young man with sharp, alert eyes who hadn't been there during Daniel's reconnaissance.

Daniel's training, his discipline, dissolved into pure instinct. He shoved the guard, hard, and ran.

The chase was short, brutal, and humiliating. He burst out of the store and onto the crowded sidewalk, but he only made it half a block before another guard, alerted by radio, tackled him from the side. He hit the pavement hard, the air knocked from his lungs, the strap of his bag digging into his shoulder.

The cold bite of the handcuffs on his wrists, the metallic tang of fear in his mouth, the profound shame of being pinned to the dirty concrete with dozens of strangers staring down at him—it was a visceral shock. The game had suddenly, violently, ended.

He was led back through the store, past the curious, accusing eyes of the shoppers, and into a small, windowless office. The police arrived minutes later. He didn't speak, didn't resist. He was a ghost again, but a different kind. A ghost in the system.

In the back of the police car, the memory of his father's face on that Christmas Day returned, a silent, mocking echo. He wasn't just a failure to his family; he was now a failure in the eyes of the law, a statistic, a name on a police report.

The holding cell was a concrete box that smelled of sweat and disinfectant. The heavy metal door slammed shut, the sound echoing the finality of his father's front door all those years ago. He was in a cage again. But this time, he had built it himself.

Episode 17: The Lifeline and the Break

He spent hours in the holding cell, the silence broken only by the distant shouts of other prisoners and the clang of metal doors. He was sure this was the end. He would be sent to juvenile detention, his life over before it had truly begun.

Then, a miracle. Or something like it. The cell door opened, and a guard told him someone was there for him. He was led to the front desk, and standing there, her face etched with a deep, weary concern, was Bertha Jo Herriott. Her presence was a stark, floral-scented contrast to the grim, disinfected surroundings of the police station.

She had gotten a call from Mr. Henderson, who, after not seeing Daniel for several days, had made some calls of his own, his worry overriding his desire not to interfere. Bertha Jo had come without hesitation. She spoke in low, calm tones to the officers, signed a series of papers, and in a blur of procedure that Daniel didn't understand, she bailed him out.

Walking out of the station and into the cool night air felt like being reborn.

"This is a one-time thing, Daniel," she said, her eyes piercing his as they stood on the sidewalk. "Teddy speaks so highly of the boy you were. He said you were kind and sweet. I won't let this mistake ruin his future by having his brother in jail."

The words stung more than any punishment. *His future*. She was protecting Teddy, not him. The act of kindness felt conditional, a shield for the brother who had followed the rules, not the one who had broken them. It reminded him of the open door to her family home that he, like Chief, had never felt worthy enough to walk through.

Still, the intervention resonated deeply. It was a crack of light in his dark world, but it also reinforced a dangerous idea: the system had cracks, and with the right help, you could slip through them.

Life on the streets continued, but the game had changed. The thrill was gone, replaced by a gnawing paranoia. Every approaching siren, every lingering glance from a stranger, felt like a threat. The constant adrenaline of the scores, the fear of being caught again, the gnawing hunger for *more*—it all began to fray the edges of his sanity. There were days of manic energy, where he felt invincible, followed by dark, suffocating periods of despair. Sleep became elusive as his thoughts raced, disjointed and sharp.

He saw his full brother, Chief, from a distance sometimes, a ghost navigating his own chaotic path, in and out of trouble. Daniel watched with a mix of concern and detached observation, now understanding the deep well of pain from which Chief's recklessness sprang. He knew that sometimes hitting rock bottom was the only way to bounce back.

Daniel's own rock bottom was approaching fast. One night, after a particularly intense period of planning and executing a series of high-stakes break-ins, something inside him snapped. The world around him seemed to distort. Colors became painfully bright, bleeding into each other like wet paint. The normal sounds of the city became a cacophony of scraping metal and sharp, piercing shrieks. Paranoia consumed him. He believed he was being followed, that every person on the street was watching him, their eyes burning into his back.

He ran, aimlessly, through the night, his mind a whirlwind of fear and delusion, convinced that shadows were reaching out to grab him. The police found him in a public park at dawn, disoriented and terrified, screaming at things only he could see. This time, they didn't take him to a holding cell. They took him to the Centre for Addiction and Mental Health.

Episode 18: The Crucible

He spent seven months at the Centre for Addiction and Mental Health. The first six were a blur of hushed voices, soft restraints, and the dull ache of medication. The chaotic symphony of the streets was replaced by the quiet, sterile routine of the institution: therapy sessions where he spoke in monosyllables, group meetings where he listened to the broken stories of others, and long, empty hours spent staring at the ceiling.

The experience humbled him, stripped him of the manic energy and perceived invincibility that had fueled his downfall. The paranoia receded, the piercing sounds faded, and the world slowly sharpened back into focus. He was diagnosed with a psychotic break, a temporary but terrifying descent into madness. In the sterile quiet of CAMH, during his slow recovery, he found a strange, distant peace. He would later learn that Chief, now a devout Christian, had been praying for him relentlessly—a spiritual tether across the city that Daniel was unaware of but that, he would come to believe, had helped pull him back from the abyss.

His mind began to clear, but the ambition remained, dormant but not dead. It was in the final month, as the doctors began to speak of his release, that the reality of his situation began to crystallize. He would be discharged into a transitional housing program with nothing but the clothes on his back. He had no money, no home, and now, a psychiatric record to go along with his criminal one. The old, familiar feeling of powerlessness, the one that had driven him to steal a pack of noodles, began to creep back in. He had been given a second chance, but it felt like a second chance at being a victim.

It was then, in the quiet hours of his last few weeks, that he began to think about the future. He replayed scenes from the true-crime movies he and Chief used to watch. He remembered the adrenaline, the precision, the respect commanded by the crews on screen. He thought of the heist scene from *Dead Presidents*. The armored truck.

The idea took root not as a fantasy, but as a solution. A logical, albeit terrifying, answer to an impossible problem. Shoplifting was a game for desperate boys. He was a man now, a man who understood risk and reward on a much deeper level.

It wasn't just about the money anymore. It was about a statement. A score so audacious, so perfectly executed, it would silence all the ghosts of his past. It would prove, once and for all, that he was not a victim, not a charity case, not a ghost at the second table. He would be the master of his own fate. The architect of his own life. The game was about to change, and this time, he would be the one making the rules.

Episode 19: Assembling the Crew

Released from CAMH into a transitional housing program, a halfway point between institutional care and the harsh realities of the street, Daniel began to move with a new, quiet purpose. He was an observer, a predator scanning the herd. The program was filled with men like him—men with fractured pasts and uncertain futures, men who were either running from something or desperately searching for a way back in. Daniel was looking for a third type: men who were ready to build something new, even if it was outside the law.

His first targets were the Abdoulkader brothers, Jabourou and Nasser. They were also navigating the system, their stories different but their sense of being on the outside the same. Daniel watched them for weeks. Jabourou, the older brother, was sharp, with a quiet intensity that matched Daniel's own. He was methodical, observant, a man who could be trusted in a tight spot. Nasser was the younger, more hot-headed one, a whirlwind of nervous energy and reckless bravado. They were two sides of the same coin: Jabourou was the mind, Nasser the muscle. They were perfect.

Daniel approached them one evening in the common area of the halfway house. He didn't come with a grand speech or a detailed blueprint. He came with a question.

"What's your plan?" he asked, sitting down at their table, his voice low and even.

Jabourou looked up, his eyes wary. "What do you mean, 'plan'?"

"For after this," Daniel said, gesturing vaguely at the drab room around them. "You going to get a job washing dishes? Stocking shelves? Is that the life you want?"

Nasser bristled. "What's it to you?"

Daniel ignored him, his gaze fixed on Jabourou. "I've seen you. You're smart. You're careful. But you're stuck. Both of you. You're playing a game that's rigged against you. I'm putting together a new game. One with better rules."

He didn't mention armored trucks or heists. He spoke of "opportunities," of "taking control," of "a score big enough to change everything." He was selling not a crime, but a philosophy—the same one that had taken root in his own mind in the sterile quiet of CAMH.

Jabourou listened, his expression unreadable. Nasser watched, a flicker of greedy excitement in his eyes.

"We're listening," Jabourou said finally.

And with those two words, the crew was born. The foundation was laid, not with bricks and mortar, but with the shared, quiet desperation of men who had decided that if the world wouldn't give them a place at the table, they would build their own.

Episode 20: The Specialists

With the Abdoulkader brothers as his foundation, Daniel began to look for the other essential pieces of his machine. He knew that brute force was not enough; he needed precision, skill, and specialized knowledge. He needed a technician and a driver.

He found Fabian Green through the city's quiet criminal grapevine. Fabian was a legend in certain circles, a man with a reputation for being able to open any lock, bypass any alarm, and handle any piece of electronics with a surgeon's steady hand. He wasn't a thug; he was a craftsman.

Daniel met him in a quiet, dimly lit bar in a forgotten part of the city. Fabian was a small, almost invisible man, with intelligent eyes that seemed to take in everything at once.

"I hear you're the best," Daniel said, sitting down opposite him, no preamble, no small talk.

Fabian took a slow sip of his beer. "The best at what?"

"At solving problems," Daniel replied. "I have a problem that requires a very specific set of tools. A problem that is... lucrative."

Fabian studied him for a long moment. "I'm retired."

"No, you're not," Daniel said, his voice calm and certain. "You're bored. You're a master craftsman with no masterpiece to build. I'm offering you a cathedral."

A flicker of interest in Fabian's eyes. "I'm listening."

Next was the driver. For that, he needed Jerome "Watts" Watson-Jibril. Watts was a getaway driver, a man who knew the city's labyrinthine streets, its hidden alleys and its traffic patterns, as if he had designed them himself. He had a reputation for being calm, unflappable, and impossibly fast.

Daniel found Watts in a garage where he worked on souped-up cars, the air thick with the smell of oil and gasoline.

"I need a driver," Daniel said, walking up to him.

Watts wiped his greasy hands on a rag and looked Daniel up and down. "Lots of people need drivers. I drive cars, not people."

"I need you to drive a route that doesn't exist on any map," Daniel said. "A route that requires you to be in exactly the right place at exactly the right time, and then to disappear. I'm told you're the only man in the city who can do it."

Watts smirked, a flash of pride in his eyes. "The city's a big place."

"And the score is a big score," Daniel countered. "Big enough that you'll never have to work in this garage again."

Watts stopped wiping his hands. He leaned against the car, his smirk replaced by a look of serious consideration. "Tell me more."

The core of the operational crew was now in place. The muscle, the technician, the driver. Each man a specialist, a master of his craft, brought together by a shared desire for something more than the world was willing to give them. Daniel wasn't just building a crew; he was building an army.

Episode 21: The Final Pieces

The operational crew was a well-oiled machine of quiet professionals. But Daniel knew that to hit the kinds of targets he was aiming for, he needed a different kind of soldier. He needed a face, a cover story, a way to walk through the front door.

He found his first piece in Jason Forget. Jason was ambitious, with a quiet, unsettling confidence and a desperate hunger to build a life for his partner, Nadine, and their young child. Daniel met them together in a crowded coffee shop, a deliberate choice to see them in their natural dynamic.

He saw the fierce, protective love in Jason's eyes, but he also saw the exhaustion in Nadine's. She was sharp, observant, and weary of their struggle. Daniel felt an immediate, dangerous pull toward her. He saw a survivor, like him.

He laid out a version of the plan, speaking not of violence or risk, but of financial freedom, of a single score that would guarantee their child's future. "This isn't about being criminals," Daniel said, his voice low and intense. "It's about being parents. It's about giving your family the life they deserve, the life the world won't let you earn."

He saw the hook land. Jason leaned forward, his eyes gleaming with ambition. But Daniel directed his next words to Nadine. "It would require a smart, observant person to make sure everything looks right. Someone people trust."

He saw the way Jason's hand rested on Nadine's arm, a subtle gesture of ownership. He saw the way Nadine watched him, Daniel, with a cautious curiosity. A new, more dangerous game began to layer itself over the heists: a subtle rivalry with Jason, fought with glances and coded words. They were in.

The final recruit was Anthea Free, a beautiful, enigmatic woman whose entire life had been an exercise in playing a part. She moved through the city's upscale circles with an easy grace, but her eyes held a cynical, world-weary intelligence. Daniel needed her to be their legitimate cover, the key that could unlock any door.

He met her for drinks at a high-end hotel bar, a place where she was clearly a regular.

"I've been told you're looking for an investor for a... creative venture," she said, looking him over, a small, knowing smile on her lips.

"I'm looking for a partner," Daniel corrected. "Someone who can walk into a bank, look a manager in the eye, and be so utterly believable that no one would ever question her presence."

"I've played many parts," she said with a cynical laugh. "Being a boring rich girl with too much money is the easiest one. My whole life was practice for it. But this part sounds expensive. And dangerous."

"The most rewarding parts always are," Daniel replied.

She took a long sip of her martini, her eyes appraising him over the rim of the glass. "Alright, Daniel," she said finally. "You have my attention. Let's hear about this cathedral you're building."

The crew was complete. The muscle, the specialists, the face. It was a perfect, deadly machine. But in assembling the final, human pieces, Daniel had also imported the very things that could cause it all to rust and break: love, jealousy, and betrayal.

Episode 22: The First Heist

The plan was a thing of beauty, a complex piece of machinery with interlocking parts. The target was a small bank branch in Montreal, far enough from home to provide a layer of anonymity. They called it the "early bird" plan, designed to strike in the quiet, vulnerable moments after the bank opened but before it was fully staffed and busy.

The operation began with Anthea. Dressed in a chic business suit, a picture of effortless wealth, she walked into the bank a week before the planned heist. She spoke to the manager about opening a safety deposit box for her "valuables," her performance so utterly believable that she was given a tour of the facilities. Her eyes, sharp and intelligent, recorded everything: camera placements, the number of staff, the location of the vault. She was their key.

On the day of the heist, they moved with the quiet confidence of professionals. Watts parked the getaway car in a pre-scouted alley a block away. Anthea, in a different car, sat across the street, a spotter on a high-tech earpiece, confirming the arrival of the two morning tellers and the manager.

"The birds are in the nest," she murmured into her mic. "You are clear."

That was the signal. Daniel, Jabourou, Nasser, and Fabian, their faces obscured by ski masks, exited their vehicle and walked calmly toward the bank's entrance. They didn't run; they moved with a purpose that was more intimidating than any frantic rush.

They burst through the doors, a brutal ballet of surgical precision.

"Nobody move!" Daniel's voice was a calm, authoritative command that cut through the morning quiet.

The three bank employees froze, their faces masks of terror. Fabian went straight for the silent alarm panel under the counter, disabling it with a few deft snips of a wire cutter. Jabourou, a silent, imposing presence, herded the employees into the back room.

Nasser, his eyes wide with a violent energy, was on the tellers, his weapon held with a white-knuckled grip. "The money! Now!" he hissed, his voice a dangerous whisper.

They were in and out in under five minutes, their bags heavy with cash. They walked, not ran, back to their car and slipped into

Montreal's morning traffic, just another anonymous vehicle on a busy street.

In the getaway car, the adrenaline was a palpable force. Nasser was buzzing, tapping his foot, replaying the moment of dominance. "Did you see their faces?" he laughed, a little too loud.

But Daniel, watching the road, noticed something else. He saw the way Jason's hands trembled on the steering wheel as he drove them to the second switch car. He saw the way Nasser's eyes were still too wide, his energy not just excited, but volatile.

The first heist was a success. A perfect score. But as they drove away, leaving the city behind, Daniel felt a cold knot of unease. His perfect machine had performed flawlessly, but he had seen the first, hairline cracks in its human parts.

Episode 23: The Midday Mayhem

The success of the Montreal job filled the crew with a dangerous confidence. They were good, and they knew it. But Daniel understood that complacency was a killer. Their "early bird" strategy was effective, but predictable. To stay ahead of the game, they needed to be able to operate in chaos. He called the new approach "The Midday Mayhem."

"Think of it like a magician's trick," Daniel explained to the crew one night, a map of downtown Toronto spread out on their safe house table. "The hand is quicker than the eye. We don't want to be invisible this time. We want to be a spectacle. We want them to be looking at a completely different show."

Their target was a busy bank in the heart of the financial district, a place that was always bustling with people, especially during the lunch hour. The plan was intricate and relied on perfect timing.

Anthea's role was different this time. Dressed in a simple, unassuming outfit, she was a watcher, a spotter, sitting in a car across the street from the bank. Her job was to give the signal the moment the street was at its peak of activity.

The distraction was the key. Watts, the driver, would create a staged, non-violent accident on the busy street directly in front of the bank. Not a serious crash, but a fender bender, enough to draw a crowd, to bring traffic to a halt, to pull the attention of the bank's security guard and every patron inside.

As Watts and a hired accomplice feigned outrage, shouting at each other and blocking the street, the rest of the crew made their move. Daniel, Jabourou, and Nasser, their faces now covered by simple bandanas instead of ski masks to appear more like opportunistic thugs than professional robbers, walked casually into the bank. They blended in with the crowd of curious onlookers peering out the windows. The bank, in a state of mild pandemonium, was an easy target.

The heist itself was a blur of quiet, practiced efficiency.

"Everyone down! Nobody move!" Daniel had shouted, his voice echoing in the sudden silence as the patrons turned from the window. "Give us the money, and nobody gets hurt!"

They moved with a calm that was more terrifying than any shouting. They were in and out in under two minutes, grabbing cash from the tellers and the back safe. The crowd outside was too focused on the staged accident to notice the three men walking briskly out of the bank with heavy bags. They slipped into a different getaway car, driven by Fabian, parked discreetly in a nearby alley.

As they drove away, they could see Watts and the other driver still arguing, a perfect, theatrical distraction that had allowed them to pull off another perfect score. The Midday Mayhem was a success. Daniel had proven he could control not just the quiet moments, but the chaos too. His confidence soared, but with it came a dangerous sense of invincibility, a hubris that was beginning to blind him to the ever-widening cracks in his crew.

Episode 24: The Vancouver Job

The damp, salty air of Vancouver felt charged with tension before they even began. The plan for the small, independent bank in the city's financial district was, on paper, flawless. But the real world, as Daniel was learning, was messy, and the crew's confidence had curdled into a dangerous recklessness.

The heist began as planned. Anthea charmed her way in and out, confirming the intel. The crew burst in, a whirlwind of adrenaline and shouted commands. But then, the hiccup. A new security guard, a middle-aged man with a kind face and a nervous twitch, was just returning from his lunch break. He saw the scene unfold and, in a moment of panicked heroism, pulled out his phone.

Nasser and Jason, seeing the same thing, reacted with impulsive violence. They ran toward the man, their guns raised, snarls on their faces.

In a moment of pure, unadulterated clarity, Daniel screamed, his voice a whip crack of command that cut through the chaos. "No! Don't shoot him! Grab the phone!"

His cold logic startled Nasser and Jason, breaking their violent focus. The man, in his panic, dropped his phone, and it skittered across the polished floor. Fabian, ever the cool-headed technician, stepped in, scooped up the phone, and shoved the terrified man into the back room with the others. The whole exchange lasted no more than ten seconds, but it felt like an eternity. The clock was ticking, the plan was off-kilter, and the air was thick with the scent of a near-disaster.

They finished the robbery, their movements frantic and sloppy now, their once-perfect rhythm shattered. In the getaway car, the silence was different this time. There was no exhilaration, no sense of triumph. There was only the quiet, simmering tension between Daniel's cold calculation and the crew's hot-headed impulsiveness.

"What were you thinking?" Daniel hissed at Jason and Nasser, his voice low and dangerous as they sped away. "No violence. That's the first rule! That's how we stay invisible!"

"He was gonna call the cops!" Jason shot back, his face flushed with adrenaline and resentment. "You want to play it cool from the back, but sometimes cool gets you caught! We were handling it."

"Handling it? You were about to commit murder for a phone!" Daniel retorted, his eyes locking with Jason's. "Emotional gets us a life sentence. You need to control yourself."

Daniel knew Jason's defensiveness was fueled by more than just the job. He could feel the unspoken accusation in Jason's eyes—an accusation about Nadine, about respect, about leadership. The seed of doubt planted in that Toronto coffee shop had taken root in Vancouver, and its bitter fruit was beginning to poison them all.

Episode 25: Buried Treasure

The near-disaster in Vancouver sobered them, but it didn't unite them. They had too much cash, a hot, heavy burden that was tangible proof of their crimes. It needed to disappear. Back in Toronto, Daniel devised a plan to bury the bulk of it in a remote patch of forest in northern Ontario, a place he'd found on a satellite map.

"Like pirate treasure?" Jason had scoffed during the tense planning meeting, his skepticism a constant, low hum of dissent. But he went along. The logic was undeniable.

The trip was a long, silent drive north. Daniel and Jabourou rode in one car, Jason and Nasser in another. The air between the two vehicles felt thick with unspoken resentment. They dug for hours under the dense canopy of ancient trees, their hands raw and blistered. The act of burying the money, sealed in waterproof bags inside large plastic tubs, felt like a funeral. They were burying their risk, but also a future. When they were finished, the air felt lighter, but in its place was the new, heavy weight of a shared, secret map.

With the immediate problem solved, the remaining proceeds from their heists funded a lifestyle of staggering excess. Daniel, who had once scrounged for instant noodles, now drove a black Mercedes-Benz C-Class, purchased with cash under a false name. He wore a heavy, gleaming Rolex on his wrist, a constant, tangible reminder of his victories. This newfound swagger, this carefully constructed facade of success, began to attract a different kind of attention.

Women, drawn to his quiet confidence and the unmistakable aura of wealth, began to gravitate toward him. He, who had once been the invisible boy, was now the center of attention. The attention was intoxicating, a drug more potent than the adrenaline of the heists themselves. It fed a deep-seated need for recognition, a craving for a place in a world that had, for so long, refused to acknowledge him.

And he used that charm, that power, to subtly continue his dangerous game with Nadine. When the crew would meet, with her sometimes present, he would direct a question to her, include her in a way that subtly excluded Jason, or share a look of understanding that was meant for her alone. He was chipping away at Jason's confidence, not with brute force, but with the quiet, corrosive power of suggestion. He was proving he could take whatever he wanted, and he was making sure Jason knew it.

Episode 26: The Hubris and the Betrayal

The armored truck plan was Daniel's magnum opus, the grand, cinematic gesture he'd been dreaming of since his time in CAMH. He watched the heist scene from *Dead Presidents* obsessively, planning every detail, every angle, every second. But the camaraderie of the crew had fully curdled into a toxic mix of fear and resentment, all of it centered on the silent war between Daniel and Jason.

The final confrontation happened in their safe house, a sterile condo overlooking the lake. It wasn't an explosion; it was a low, venomous exchange that sealed their fate.

"I see how you look at her," Jason finally said, his voice trembling with a rage he could no longer contain. He had just seen Daniel share a quiet laugh with Nadine by the window, a small, intimate moment that felt like a deliberate provocation. "You think I'm stupid? You walk in here with your fancy car and your big plans, and you think you can just take what's mine?"

Daniel turned, his expression one of cold, condescending calm. "This isn't about Nadine," he replied, his voice a tone that was more insulting than a shout. "This is about the job. And you're too emotional for it. You're a liability."

"A liability?" Jason's voice cracked. "I'm the one with a family to lose! A kid! What do you have? Nothing! What do you care if it all goes wrong?"

It was a fatal miscalculation on Daniel's part. In his supreme hubris, he felt a divine ownership over the armored truck plan. He couldn't tolerate a challenge to his authority, especially not from the man he was quietly cuckolding.

"You're done," Daniel said, his voice flat and final, a judge delivering a sentence. "You're off the crew. This is a game of chess, Jason. And you're not a player."

He turned his back on Jason, a gesture of ultimate dismissal. He had cast aside the wrong man. Broken, humiliated, and terrified of losing his family to the charismatic ghost who had stolen his place, Jason Forget walked out of the condo. He sat in his car for an hour, the city lights blurring through his tears. He thought of his child, of Nadine's worried eyes, of the dead-end life that awaited him if he was cut out. Then he drove, not home, but to a police station. In a bitter, desperate act of revenge, he told them everything.

Episode 27: The Unraveling and the Sting

The police knew. They had been watching for weeks, their intelligence a direct result of Jason Forget's vengeful tip. They had a team of armed officers waiting, a cold, silent audience to a scene they knew was about to unfold. The suburban street was quiet, the air thick with the humidity of an overcast summer day. They were in position, a meticulously choreographed operation waiting for its cue.

Daniel, unaware of the net closing around him, was consumed by his vision. He, Jabourou, Nasser, Fabian, Watts, and Anthea sat in a rented van, parked discreetly down the street from the bank. They wore ski masks and dark clothes, the only visible skin around their eyes. In the back, resting ominously, was the large, industrial garbage bin.

It was a perfect echo of the movie. Daniel had studied the scene frame by frame, analyzing the angles, the timing, the movements. As the armored truck pulled up, his heart hammered a frantic rhythm against his ribs. This was it. The moment of truth.

Jabourou, acting as the decoy, began to unload the garbage bin, struggling with its weight and feigning clumsiness. It was a perfect, mundane distraction. The guards, their attention briefly diverted, stepped out of the truck.

"Now!" Daniel hissed into his earpiece.

This was their cue. Daniel, Nasser, and Watts moved with swift, practiced efficiency. They burst from the back of the van, weapons drawn, shouting commands. "On the ground! Now! Don't move!" The scene was chaotic, a blur of motion and terror. They were the masters of their domain, for a fleeting moment, in control of their destiny.

But this isn't a movie, and the audience was far from passive. The moment Daniel and Nasser burst from the van, the police moved. Sirens, previously silent, began to wail, a high-pitched scream that cut through the mundane quiet of the street. Officers swarmed from all sides, their weapons drawn, a dozen red laser dots appearing on Daniel's chest, his head, his hands. This wasn't a robbery in progress; it was a sting operation, a net that had been carefully laid and was now being pulled tight.

"Police! Drop your weapons!" an officer bellowed through a bullhorn. "On the ground! Hands where we can see them!"

Daniel, his mind a whirlwind of confusion and adrenaline, knew they were finished. He saw the cold, hard eyes of the police, the glint of their weapons, and the game he had been playing all these years came to a sudden, brutal halt. There was no escape this time, no Bertha Jo to bail him out. He dropped his weapon, his hands raised, the cold reality of a world without a script crashing down on him.

Episode 28: The Verdict

The court case that followed was a blur of legal jargon, a sterile, dispassionate recounting of the chaotic events that had defined the past few years of his life. He sat in court, a spectator to his own story, listening to the charges being laid out: four counts of armed robbery, one count of attempted robbery, and a host of weapons charges. The document he would later read, a dry, factual account of his life's trajectory, would lay it all bare.

His lawyer, a tired but earnest public defender, argued the facts with a quiet ferocity. The prosecutor, a young woman with a sharp mind and an even sharper suit, painted a picture of a criminal mastermind, a man who had orchestrated a series of violent, cross-country robberies. Daniel, sitting in the defendant's chair, felt a strange sense of detachment. He had lived this life, but the person they were describing felt like a stranger, a caricature of the man he had become.

The judge, a stern but fair woman, listened to all of it, her face a mask of impartial observation. The verdict came down, a quiet, deliberate recitation of the facts. The judge would stay the first count but find him guilty on counts two through eight—the bank robberies that had been their bread and butter.

But the charges related to the armored truck, the grand, cinematic gesture that had failed so spectacularly, would be a different matter. The defense argued that the evidence was circumstantial, the link between the gun and the robbery tenuous, and that there was no conclusive proof that he had altered the serial number on the weapon.

In a surprising turn, the judge ruled in his favor, finding him not guilty on that specific charge.

It was a small, ironic victory, a hollow comfort in the face of the long prison sentence that awaited him. He had been acquitted of his dream but convicted of his reality. He was no longer a phantom, a player in a game of his own making. He was simply a man, sitting in a courtroom, a prisoner of his own ambition. The uncharted path he had chosen had led him, not to freedom, but to a cell, a place where he would have to finally confront the ghosts of his past and the long, silent journey that lay ahead.

Episode 29: The Weight of Solitude

The clanging of the metal door echoed behind him, a sound of absolute finality. The world he had known—the frantic rush of the city, the adrenaline-fueled heists, the quiet desperation of the streets— was gone, replaced by the stark, unrelenting reality of a concrete cell. The air, thick with the smell of disinfectant and stale humanity, was a world away from the fleeting taste of triumph he had chased. Daniel was no longer a player in a game; he was a statistic, a number, a man defined by the cold, hard walls that now enclosed him.

He served his time, a seven-year blur of monotonous routine and internal reflection. The years were a crucible, burning away the manic energy of his past and leaving behind a quieter, more hardened man. He read, he thought, he observed. The ghosts of his past—his father's absence, his brothers' departure, Teddy's unyielding discipline—retained their power, but they no longer held the same grip on him. He was no longer running from them; he was simply living with their weight.

His brother, Chief, found him shortly after his release. He was a different man now, a devout Christian who saw Daniel's release not as the end of a prison sentence, but as the beginning of a spiritual one. They met in a small, sterile coffee shop, the air smelling of burnt coffee and sugar.

"I prayed for you every day," Chief said, his eyes filled with a raw, earnest love that made Daniel deeply uncomfortable. "Every single day, I told God to watch over you, to bring you back to us."

"I'm out now, Chief," Daniel said, his voice a flat monotone. "I'm back."

"You're back in body, but your spirit is still in there," Chief replied, his voice thick with emotion. "I can see it. The darkness is still in you." He spoke of the shock and sadness that Daniel's path had caused, how incomprehensible it was for the sweet, gentle boy he had grown up with to have become this man. "I keep thinking about those A&E shows we used to watch, you know?" Chief said, his voice dropping to a whisper. "The gangster stories. We thought it was just a game. A movie. I keep wondering if it's my fault, if we put that idea in your head."

But Daniel, after seven years of silent, solitary thought, was not ready to be saved. He had found his own brand of salvation in the silence: a defiant self-reliance born of his own mistakes. He loved his brother, but he couldn't walk his path. To embrace Chief's world would mean dismantling the quiet peace he had so carefully constructed.

Chief, with a painful clarity, understood. "I'll always be here for you," he said, his voice thick with unshed tears. "When you're ready, I'll be here."

Daniel watched him go. He felt no tears this time, only the cold, hard weight of his own choice. He was free, yes, but he was also, truly, alone. The ghost that haunted him most, however, was not one of damnation, but of discipline. Teddy. The brother who was not dead, but "dead to him." He held a secret hope, a quiet, desperate longing that one day, they might be able to reconcile.

Episode 30: The Weight of a Son

The quiet peace Daniel had found in his solitude was shattered the day he saw the ultrasound picture. It was an accident, a brief, chaotic encounter at a government office where he was reporting to his parole officer. Sarah, a woman from his transitional housing program he had known for a few short months before his sentence, was there, a form in her hand, her belly round with life.

She saw the shock on his face and held up the small, grainy photo. She hadn't known how to contact him. He had been a ghost, a name on a piece of paper, and she had moved on, building a new life for herself and the child.

But Daniel was back. And the child was his.

His son, Elijah, was born a few months later, a small, perfect being who was a constant, living rebuke to the wasted years of his past. He wasn't born into a grand, cinematic life of crime and ambition; he was born into the quiet, humble reality of a small, two-bedroom apartment that Sarah had scraped together. They weren't a conventional couple; they were co-parents, bound by a shared responsibility to a life neither of them had fully planned for.

Daniel worked relentlessly to be a part of it. He had a debt to the system, a deep financial obligation in the form of restitution for the bank robberies. It was a shadow that followed him everywhere, a constant reminder of the lives he had disrupted. The court had ordered a payment plan, a slow, agonizing process. But now, he was determined. It was a new form of discipline, a penance for his past, and a driving force for his future.

He found his calling in a way he never expected. He started a small-scale junk removal and landscaping business. He worked alone at first, the physical labor—hauling away discarded furniture, cutting overgrown lawns, tearing out weeds—a cathartic release from the mental prisons he had once built for himself. He saw the satisfaction in a clean lawn, a cleared-out garage, a space made new again. The work was honest, the pay was fair, and it allowed him a kind of freedom he had never known before.

As his business grew, he hired a few men, others like him who were trying to find their footing after a prison sentence. He was a good boss, fair but firm, the lessons from his brother Teddy's unyielding discipline now serving him in a positive way. He knew what it was like to be judged, and he gave his men the one thing he had never received: a second chance with a new set of rules.

The greatest joy in his life, however, was Elijah. The boy was a bright, curious child, with his mother's wide eyes and his father's quiet, observant nature. Daniel would spend hours with him, reading to him, teaching him to catch a ball, building things out of Lego. These simple, beautiful moments were a world away from the violence and paranoia of his past. He never spoke of his time in prison, never spoke of the life he had once lived. But the lessons were there in his every action: the relentless work ethic, the quiet patience, and the deep, unyielding love he had for this small life he was responsible for.

Episode 31: Unspoken Truths

The peace Daniel had found in his new life was a fragile one, constantly haunted by the ghost of his past, especially the memory of his brother, Teddy. One evening, after putting Elijah to bed, the phone rang. It was an unfamiliar number with a California area code. Daniel hesitated, then answered.

"Daniel?" The voice was a ghost from his past, older but unmistakable. "It's Teddy."

A thousand emotions flooded Daniel at once: shock, anger, resentment, and a deep, buried relief. He hadn't heard that voice in decades, and it brought back the raw pain of their final parting.

"Teddy," Daniel said, his voice flat, a mask he had perfected over the years.

There was a long silence on the other end. "I'm sorry I didn't call sooner. I got your number from Bertha Jo," Teddy finally said. "I... I just wanted to tell you I'm sorry." The apology was a physical thing, a weight lifting from Daniel's shoulders that he hadn't known was there.

"I know you have two girls now," Daniel said, his voice softer now. "I saw them once, before I went away. And I saw you at the courthouse with the younger one, Anna Lisa. I remember her wide eyes." The memory was a shard of glass in his mind—seeing a vision of the family he had lost from behind the barrier of his own destruction, a ghost watching ghosts. "I heard Anna Lisa is studying to be an oncologist and Eva Maria is in her final year of Nursing in USC San Diego."

Teddy's voice broke with emotion. "Yes. That's... that's my girls. They're good kids. I'm so proud of them. I'm... I'm so sorry I wasn't there for you, Daniel. I was too hard on you. I was a child myself, trying to be a man."

"I have a son now, too," Daniel said, the words tumbling out before he could stop them. "His name is Elijah." He told Teddy about his business, about the quiet life he had built for himself. He spoke not with pride, but with a quiet sense of ownership, of a life he had earned.

"That's wonderful, Daniel," Teddy said, his voice unwavering. "I... I would love for you all to come to California. There's a room here for you. We can... we can just talk."

The offer, meant to be a kindness, hung in the air like a ghost. Daniel's peace was instantly shattered, replaced by the bitter, cold reality of his past. The criminal conviction, the one that had allowed him to walk free in Canada, was also a lock, a barrier that he couldn't cross.

"Teddy," Daniel said, his voice barely a whisper. "I can't. I... I can't cross the border."

There was a moment of silence on the other end of the line, a sudden, brutal understanding. "Your record," Teddy said, his voice heavy with a profound sadness. "Of course. I'm so sorry."

"Don't be," Daniel said, his voice firmer now. "It is what it is. I made my choices. This is part of the price."

"Then I'll come to you," Teddy said, his voice unwavering. "I'll come to Toronto. We can talk. We can meet. We'll find a way."

The conversation ended with a promise to call again, a fragile, new thread of connection after a lifetime of severance. Daniel hung up the phone, a strange mixture of emotions swirling inside him. He looked at the family photo on the fridge: Sarah, with her kind smile; Elijah, with his bright eyes; and himself, a man who had finally found his place. His mother was a world away in Guadalajara, and his brother was a world away in California, but for the first time, those distances felt like miles, not chasms. The weight of his son was a heavy one, but it was an anchor, not a chain. It was a weight that had finally set him free, and given him the courage to face the echoes of his past. He had walked an uncharted path, but he had, at last, found his way home.

End.